COLORFUL
MINDS

TIPS FOR
MANAGING
YOUR EMOTIONS

FUSION

The Yellow Book

What to Do When You're Excited

by
William Anthony

BEARPORT
PUBLISHING

Minneapolis, Minnesota

Credits

Cover and throughout – Ekaterina Kapranova, Beatriz Gascon J. 4 – NLshop. 7 – My Portfolio, Nikolaeva. 8 – studiovin. 10 – Coprid. 11 – Katya Kandalova. 12 – janrysavy. 13 – Diego Schtutman. 14 – alikemalkarasu. 15 – grmarc, Nadezda Barkova. 16 – Team Ok-topus. 17 – Andrei310, DusanBartolovic. 20 – alexmak7. 22 – NLshop. Additional illustrations by Danielle Webster-Jones. All images courtesy of shutterstock. com. With thanks to Getty Images, Thinkstock Photo and iStockphoto.

Library of Congress Cataloging-in-Publication Data is available at www.loc.gov or upon request from the publisher.

ISBN: 978-1-64747-581-9 (hardcover)
ISBN: 978-1-64747-586-4 (paperback)
ISBN: 978-1-64747-591-8 (ebook)

© 2022 Booklife Publishing

This edition is published by arrangement with Booklife Publishing.

For more information, write to Bearport Publishing, 5357 Penn Avenue South, Minneapolis, MN 55419. Printed in the United States of America.

For more
The Yellow Book activities:

1. Go to **www.factsurfer.com**

2. Enter "**Yellow Book**" into the search box.

3. Click on the cover of this book
to see a list of activities.

CONTENTS

Imagine a Rainbow 4

Scavenger Hunt 6

A Chore No More 8

Tell a Tale 10

Get Energetic! 12

The Calm Zone 14

Critter Spotting 16

Super You 18

Little Ideas 20

Feeling Better? 22

Glossary 24

Index 24

IMAGINE A RAINBOW

Red is angry.

Orange is for when I feel shy.

Green is scared.

Feeling worried

The rainbow has a color for every feeling. Sometimes, one color shines brighter than the others.

4

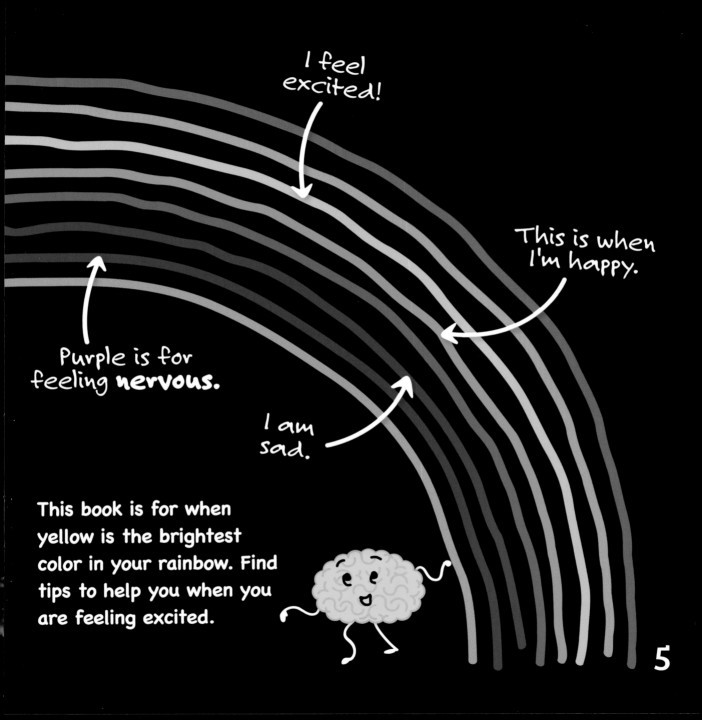

SCAVENGER HUNT

Are you ever so excited that you feel as if you are bouncing off the walls?

That's fantastic! But if we bounce too much, we might break things. So, let's **channel** that excitement with a scavenger hunt!

Place this book flat on the floor or on a table. Follow along with the scavenger hunt on the next page. Place something on every space to complete the challenge!

TOP TIP!

Stay safe! Walk, don't run!

6

TRY TO FIND . . .

SOMETHING ROUND

SOMETHING YELLOW

SOMETHING SOFT

SOMETHING TINY

SOMETHING YOU DRAW WITH

SOMETHING SQUARE

SOMETHING THAT MAKES YOU SMILE

7

A CHORE NO MORE

Sometimes we're more excited about the things we want to do than the things we have to do. It can be hard to stay **focused** on chores.

Choose something you have to do every day. Break it down into four easy steps. Write them on sticky notes or small bits of paper and place them on the squares.

Check off each step as you go. This makes it easier to stay focused!

You can choose any part of the day you'd like. Here's an example for getting ready for school!

1 Eat breakfast

2 Brush my teeth

PLACE YOUR STEPS HERE

3 Pack my bag

4 Put my shoes on

9

TELL A TALE

On some days, our minds can be full. We might get lost in daydreams or **distracted** by all the thoughts bubbling in our brains. Let's try to put some of this **creativity** into a story.

TOP TIP!

You could use a single word in a blank space or you could use 20. It's up to you!

Make a copy of the next page or find another sheet of paper to fill in the blanks!

This is the story of two kids named _____ and _____. One day, they went to the _____. They found a _____. "Amazing," they thought. "We could use this to _____!" They took it home and showed it to _____. Suddenly, something appeared. "oh no," said the children. It was a _____!

Try to keep going! What story will you tell?

GET ENERGETIC!

When we feel excited, we might feel as though we could run around the world 100 times.

It can be a good idea to get all that energy out through **exercise!**

Look at the next page. Do each exercise as many times as you need to!

TOP TIP!

Put on some high-energy music while you exercise!

STEP 1:

Run in place for 20 seconds!

STEP 2:

Do 10 jumping jacks!

STEP 3:

Do 10 big arm circles.

STEP 4:

Rest and breathe deeply for 20 seconds.

THE CALM ZONE

Being excited is amazing, but when we are too excited we can bother other people.

It's important to have a place you can go when you need to calm down. Find a quiet space and take something you can focus on, such as pencils and paper for drawing. Take 10 minutes to **relax**!

TOP TIP!

Make a sign to warn others to stay out of your calm zone.

KEEP OUT!

Someone
is using the
calm zone.

CRITTER SPOTTING

One of the best places to calm down is outside! Being in nature with lots of fresh air can help us relax.

It's also good to have something we can focus on. Look at the checklist of critters on the next page. See how many you can find while you're exploring!

TOP TIP!

Always be kind to animals. Never pick up, move, or hurt them!

Can you find . . .

A critter that
can fly?

A bug
that's green?

A bug with
six legs?

A critter
with no legs?

SUPER YOU

Sometimes, our excitement can annoy people, and they might ask us to go away. This might make us feel bad about ourselves.

When we feel like this, it is important to remember how super we are!

Get a trusted adult or friend and follow the steps on the next page together.

18

STEP 1:

Get some pencils and paper.

STEP 2:

Write or draw something you are good at or that people like about you. Don't let the other person see!

STEP 3:

At the same time, ask the other person to do the same thing about you. Don't look at their paper either!

STEP 4:

When you are both finished, show each other what makes you so super!

LITTLE IDEAS

There are lots of little tips and tricks you can use when you feel excited.

GET CREATIVE

Draw or paint something amazing!

HIT THE DANCE FLOOR

Get your body moving and dance to some awesome music!

FIDGET FRIENDS

If you feel restless and **fidgety**, try to use something small and quiet that you can squeeze, tap, or twirl in your hands.

PUZZLES

Get focused by trying a jigsaw puzzle or a puzzle book.

BUBBLE WRAP POP

Roll out a sheet of bubble wrap and walk all over it! Listen for all the little pops! Always ask an adult first.

TER?

h tip worked
for you? Why
u think
is?

If you feel calmer and more
focused, now is a good time to
think about what happened
when you got excited. Was it
super fun, or did it cause some
problems? It is important to
notice when you get too excited.

Remember, you are like everyone else. We all have colorful minds.

Every feeling you have is important!
This book will still be here

whenever

you need it.

23

GLOSSARY

channel to express your feelings, thoughts, energy, or ideas through a certain action or activity

creativity the ability to imagine, make new things, or think new thoughts

distracted unable to think about or pay attention to something

exercise movements you make to become stronger and healthier

fidgety restless and unable to sit still

focused paying close attention to something or putting effort into a task

nervous worried or afraid about what might happen

relax to stop feeling nervous or worried

INDEX

breathing 13
calm 14–16, 22
creativity 10, 20
energetic 12
exercise 12

fidgeting 21
focusing 8, 14, 16, 21–22
imagination 4, 10
relaxing 14, 16
restless 12, 21